THE BUCKLAND STORIES

On Professional Judgment

and

Consequence

Sarah K. Ellwood

Contents

The Report

Part I The Report

The Approach

Buckland read the letter twice before returning it to the envelope. The instruction had come by referral from a forensic accounting colleague he had worked with until his recent retrenchment. It was not unusual in form. The language was careful, the paper heavy without ostentation, the sender's address one he recognised immediately. The request was framed narrowly, as such requests always were, and it arrived with the familiar combination of courtesy and urgency that suggested the decision to engage him had already been taken elsewhere.

He did not open the enclosure at once. Instead, he set the letter on his desk, aligning it squarely with the edge, and turned to the window. From his office, the street looked orderly enough: traffic moving, people crossing at the lights, a delivery vehicle idling where it shouldn't be. Nothing in the view suggested difficulty. Nothing ever did.

The letter proposed a limited engagement. It specified a defined assessment date, a prescribed framework, and an opinion confined to compliance with requirements as they stood at that time. It was explicit about exclusions. No projections. No forward-looking commentary. No assessment of resilience, sustainability, or fitness beyond the period under review. The opinion would be relied upon, it said, but only for the purpose described.

Buckland returned to his chair and read the letter a third time, slower now, attending not to what was included but to what was absent. There was no attempt to disguise the narrowness of the mandate. On the contrary, it was set out with a precision that suggested prior discussion—perhaps with advisers, perhaps internally—about how far the question should be allowed to range.

He recognised the structure immediately. It was orthodox. It was defensible. It was the kind of framing that survived scrutiny precisely because it did not claim to answer more than it did.

He opened the enclosure.

The supporting material was substantial but orderly. There were schedules, certifications, extracts from the relevant framework, and a draft timetable that assumed cooperation and efficiency. Someone had taken care to assemble it. Someone had also taken care to ensure that nothing within it invited a broader inquiry.

Buckland did not yet know what the answer would be. That was immaterial at this stage. What mattered was whether the question, as framed, could be answered cleanly—and whether doing so would exhaust what needed to be said.

He placed the papers back into their order and reached for a notepad. At the top of the page, he wrote the assessment date, underlined it once, and below it the words scope and reliance. He paused, then added a third line: assumptions.

Only then did he pick up the telephone.

Scope

"Buckland."

"Yes—good afternoon, Mr Buckland. Thank you for calling back."

"I've read the letter."

"I'm glad. We were hoping the scope would be clear."

"It is," Buckland said. "Clear and narrow."

"Yes," the voice replied, quickly. "That was deliberate."

"I assumed so," Buckland said. "The opinion is to address compliance as at the assessment date only. No forward-looking analysis. No commentary beyond the framework."

"That's correct."

"And the opinion will be relied upon?"

There was a pause.

"Yes," the caller said. "For the purpose described."

Buckland did not respond immediately. He picked up the letter again, though he did not need to read it.

"I ask because reliance has a habit of travelling," he said. "Even when the language is careful."

"We understand," the caller said. "Which is why we've been precise about the exclusions."

"Indeed," Buckland said. "You will understand that precision works both ways."

"I would expect nothing less," the caller replied. The tone was warm but controlled. "We're not asking for anything outside your usual approach."

"No," Buckland said. "You're not."

"If I were to take this on," Buckland said, "the opinion would reflect the scope as written. It would not extend to matters the framework does not require to be assessed."

"That is exactly what we're looking for," the caller said. "A clean answer to a defined question."

Buckland let that stand.

"There may be some drafting discussion," the caller added, lightly. "As there always is."

"I'm sure," Buckland said.

"And of course," the caller continued, "we'd want to avoid unnecessary qualifications."

Buckland smiled, faintly.

"Unnecessary ones are easily avoided," he said.

The caller laughed, a little too readily.

"Good," he said. "Then perhaps we can proceed?"

Buckland did not answer at once.

"I'll need to review the materials properly," he said. "And confirm that the scope is workable as stated."

"Of course."

"I'll come back to you," Buckland said.

"Thank you," the caller said. "We appreciate your time."

"So do I," Buckland said, and ended the call.

He replaced the handset and sat for a moment without moving. Then he turned back to the papers and began again, more slowly this time.

Initial Review

The materials were better prepared than most.

Work of this kind tended to attract attention long before it reached his desk, and by the time it did, several layers of review had already been applied. Schedules reconciled. Certifications cross-referenced. Numbers footnoted to within an inch of their lives. Buckland worked through them methodically, marking nothing, making no notes beyond page numbers and cross-checks he would return to later.

The framework was familiar. He had worked under it often enough to know where discretion ended and convention began. The requirements were prescriptive, but not crude. They allowed judgment where judgment was unavoidable, and they permitted assumptions where proof would have been impractical or disproportionate. Systems could not function without a degree of abstraction.

By mid-afternoon he had confirmed what he had expected to find: at the assessment date, the thresholds were met. Ratios cleared their minima. Buffers were in place. The calculations followed the form required of them. If he had stopped there, the answer would already have been clear.

He did not stop there.

It was in the notes to the calculations that he first saw it—not as a flaw, and not as an omission, but as a dependency. The figures rested on an assumption that was set out plainly enough, justified by reference to historical patterns and accepted practice. It was not hidden. It did not need to be. The framework allowed it.

He turned back a page and then forward again, tracing where the assumption entered the model and how often it was relied upon thereafter. The effect was cumulative rather than dramatic. Nothing collapsed without it; nothing failed outright. But without it, the margins narrowed, and the comfort implied by the final figures became conditional.

Buckland sat back slightly in his chair, giving the numbers space.

The assumption concerned continuity—of access, of behaviour, of conditions continuing broadly as they had before. It did not assert that nothing would change, only that nothing relevant would change quickly enough to matter within the period under review. That was the logic. It was internally consistent. It had precedent.

He checked the framework again. There was no requirement to test the assumption. No obligation to ask what might happen if it failed. The calculation was to be taken as it stood, provided the assumption was reasonable at the assessment date.

And at the assessment date, it was.

He made a note this time, brief and non-committal. Not a conclusion. Just a marker, a reminder of where the work was carrying weight it did not acknowledge explicitly.

Later, as the light in the room shifted and the street outside grew quieter, he returned to the assumption once more. He compared it with the surrounding commentary, the tone of the management certifications, the way the language moved smoothly over what it depended upon.

Nothing in the file required alarm.

Buckland closed the folder and set it aside.

The answer, when he came to give it, would not turn on this point. He knew that already. The question he had been asked did not reach that far.

Still, he left the note where it was, visible on the page when he reopened the file the next morning.

Drafting

By the end of the second day, Buckland could have issued the opinion.

The calculations were complete. The thresholds were met. Cross-references aligned cleanly with the framework. There were no anomalies requiring explanation, no judgment calls that would need to be defended later. It was the kind of file that invited closure, that rewarded decisiveness.

He began a draft instead.

The first pages came together quickly. The language was familiar, almost automatic. It did not require invention, only care. Paragraph followed paragraph in the order he had used before, the conclusions narrowing naturally toward the point the engagement had been designed to reach.

Halfway through, he paused and glanced at the timetable. There was nothing unrealistic about it. If anything, it assumed more time than the work strictly required.

He saved the document and closed it without printing.

The temptation was not to cut corners. It was to finish — to give the answer while it was still uncomplicated, before the work acquired additional gravity simply by remaining open.

Over time, Buckland had learned that efficiency could become its own argument. A clean file, delivered promptly, acquired an authority that lingered even when the question it answered was narrow. Delay, by contrast, invited curiosity.

He reopened the draft and made a small change to the heading, nothing substantive.

Then he left it unfinished.

Expectation

The email arrived the following morning.

It was brief, courteous, and written as if to be helpful.

Just checking in to see whether everything is progressing as expected. We appreciate how clear the framework is in this instance and are keen to keep matters moving if possible.

There was no instruction in it. No deadline imposed. Nothing he could object to.

Buckland read it twice.

The phrase, keep matters moving, was innocuous enough, but it carried an implication he recognised. The work had become, in their minds, a formality. Something that had done its job by existing, and now merely needed to conclude.

He did not reply immediately.

When he returned to the draft, he noticed how easily it supported that expectation. The conclusions sat comfortably on the page. Read quickly, the answer felt

reassuring. There was nothing in it that demanded
interruption.

That, too, was part of the problem.

He added a comment in the margin, not to change
the conclusion, but to mark where the work rested most
heavily on what was assumed rather than shown.

Only then did he reply to the email, thanking them
for the note and confirming that the work was
proceeding.

He did not mention timing.

The Opinion

Buckland re-drafted the opinion in the morning.

He began, as he always did, with the scope. He set it out plainly, in the same language the engagement letter had used, neither narrowing nor expanding it. Dates were precise. References to the framework were exact. Nothing in the opening paragraphs invited interpretation.

The work had been done carefully, and the writing reflected that. Each conclusion was tied back to a requirement. Each requirement to a source. The structure made the document easy to follow and, just as importantly, easy to rely upon.

He paused only once, midway through the summary of work performed, to confirm a reference. Then he continued.

The compliance position emerged naturally from the analysis. There was no rhetorical emphasis, no need to underline the point. The numbers met the thresholds. The certifications supported the calculations. The framework's conditions were satisfied as at the assessment date.

He wrote the conclusion without hesitation.

On the basis of the work performed, and subject to the scope described above, I conclude that the entity complied with the applicable requirements as at the assessment date.

He read the sentence again. It was correct. It said no more than it should, and no less.

The supporting sections followed in orderly sequence. Methodology. Information relied upon. Matters not examined. Each section closed the door behind it, leaving nothing loose, nothing unresolved.

By the time he reached the final page, the document had acquired a quiet solidity. It felt finished — not because it was complete in any broader sense, but because it answered the question it had been asked with a clarity that invited acceptance.

Buckland printed the draft and laid it beside the file.

Read as a whole, it did exactly what the engagement required. It provided certainty where certainty was permitted, and silence where silence was orthodox. Anyone reading it quickly would come away reassured. Anyone reading it closely would find nothing to object to.

That, he knew, was its strength.

He marked a single paragraph with a pencil — not to change it, but to remind himself where the work depended most heavily on the assumptions the framework allowed him to take as given.

He did not alter the conclusion.

Instead, he turned back to the beginning and read the draft again, this time not as its author but as someone who would rely on it. He noted how easily the answer travelled, how little resistance the language offered to use beyond its intended purpose.

When he reached the end, he did not sign it.

He set the draft aside, straightened the papers, and opened a new document.

Reliance

The new document was blank except for the header.

Buckland typed it out of habit rather than necessity: the opinion title, the reference number, the date. He paused before copying anything across from the draft beside him.

The temptation was to add a sentence. To qualify something already said. To soften an inference at the margin.

He resisted it.

Qualifications buried in conclusions were easily missed. Worse, they could be read as hedging rather than boundary-setting. If the work was to carry a limit, it needed to carry it openly.

He scrolled back through the draft and stopped at the section dealing with reliance. It was standard language, carefully inherited and rarely questioned. He read it once, then again, this time as someone looking for permission rather than constraint.

He placed the cursor beneath it and began to type.

The first version was too long. It explained itself. He deleted it without saving.

The second was too cautious. It retreated into generalities that would protect him without protecting the work. He deleted that as well.

On the third attempt, he slowed down.

He wrote each sentence with reference to the framework, not to the file in front of him. He named no outcome. He described no risk. He allowed no speculation to enter the language.

When he reached the final line, he stopped.

The paragraph did not accuse. It did not warn. It did not challenge the conclusion that preceded it.

But it refused to travel.

Buckland read it once, and then again. He considered where to place it.

At the end, it would be polite.

In a footnote, it would be invisible.

Inserted mid-paragraph, it would look defensive.

He placed it immediately after the reliance section, before the conclusion.

Anyone reading the document in sequence would encounter it before reaching the answer. Anyone skimming would still trip over it.

That was intentional.

He saved the document under a new filename and printed the revised draft.

Read as a whole, the opinion felt different. Not weaker. More exact. The answer was still there, unchanged, but it no longer stood alone. It carried a boundary with it, one that required attention before acceptance.

Buckland signed the cover page and set the document aside for dispatch.

He considered reopening it — checking the phrasing again, weighing whether the final sentence could be softened without losing its effect.

He did not.

Instead, he shut down the computer, gathered the papers into a single stack, and placed them neatly at the corner of the desk.

The work was finished.

What would happen next was no longer his to decide.

Interpretation

Subject: Clarification of Reliance Language — Opinion dated [date]

Dear Mr Buckland,

Thank you for providing the draft opinion. We appreciate the clarity of the conclusions and the careful articulation of scope.

As part of our internal review, we would welcome clarification regarding the limitation on reliance set out in the section titled [Limitation on Reliance and Scope].

In particular, we would be grateful if you could confirm our understanding that the reference to "adverse developments that were identifiable, though not assessed" is intended solely to delineate the boundary of the work performed, rather than to suggest any specific concern or expectation beyond the assessment date.

We recognise that the opinion is confined to compliance as at that date and do not seek to extend its scope. Our intention is simply to ensure that the language is interpreted consistently by all relevant parties and relied upon only for the purpose described.

If it would assist, we would be happy to discuss this briefly by telephone.

Kind regards,

[Name]

[Title]

[Organisation]

Application

Buckland did not see the message arrive.

He found it later, when he returned to his desk after lunch and worked methodically through what had come in while he was away. Most of it he dealt with quickly. One message he opened, read once, and then left on the screen without touching the mouse.

He was copied, not addressed.

The sender was someone he did not know. The recipients included several names he recognised from the file and one he did not. The subject line referred to the matter obliquely, as if it had already acquired an internal shorthand.

Halfway down the message, a paragraph was set out separately.

As noted by Buckland in his opinion of [date], reliance on compliance is confined to the assessment date and does not extend to outcomes dependent on assumptions permitted by the framework but not tested under it. On that basis, we recommend…

Buckland read the sentence again.

It was accurate. The phrasing was not his, but the substance was faithful enough. The recommendation that followed was cautious, procedural, and entirely someone else's.

No one had asked him whether that was the correct reading.

No one had asked him whether he agreed with what followed from it.

They had moved on.

He scrolled up and looked again at the distribution list. He was the only external name. He was there for context, not contribution.

Buckland rested his hands on the edge of the desk. The sensation was not one of surprise, but of recognition. His words had travelled: detached from him, stabilised by citation, used to support decisions he did not make.

He could reply. He could clarify further. He could ask to be consulted.

All of those would require a new record.

He closed the message without responding.

For the rest of the afternoon, the file remained where it was. Other work took its place. Calls were returned. Notes were made. But the shape of the day had altered slightly, as if a weight had shifted somewhere out of sight.

Later, before shutting down, he reopened the message once more and read it through to the end.

Nothing in it was wrong.

That, he understood, was the point.

Standing

The meeting took place without him.

Buckland learned of it only because the papers appeared in his inbox later that afternoon, forwarded without comment by someone who had not attended. The covering note was brief, almost apologetic, as if to excuse the intrusion.

For awareness.

He opened the attachment.

It was a summary, not minutes. Cleanly written. Deliberately non-attributive. Decisions were described as having been "noted" or "considered," never made. Responsibility appeared only in the abstract.

His name appeared once.

Not in a heading. Not as a participant. Embedded in a paragraph dealing with external inputs.

The independent opinion provided by Buckland has been reviewed in conjunction with advice received from internal and external counsel…

There was no reference to his clarification. No quotation. Just the assurance that it had been "taken into account."

Buckland read on.

The document outlined a set of next steps that resembled preparation rather than action: further internal review, alignment of reliance language, engagement with relevant stakeholders at an appropriate time. Nothing was urgent. Nothing was final.

The opinion — his opinion — had become one element among several, its edges softened by proximity to others.

He closed the file and left it open on the desk.

Later that week, a second document arrived, this one from a different source entirely. It addressed the same matter, but in a different register — less legal, more managerial. Where the first had spoken of frameworks and scope, this one spoke of confidence and continuity.

Again, his name appeared once.

Again, he was not asked to comment.

The documents did not contradict him. They did not need to. They worked around what he had said, redistributing weight rather than removing it. The assumption he had marked was no longer central; it had become contextual.

By the end of the week, the matter had acquired a cadence. Emails referenced earlier emails. Papers referred back to summaries of discussions he had not attended. His opinion was cited in footnotes, sometimes accurately, sometimes approximately.

No one contacted him to clarify.

Buckland found that he no longer expected them to.

He returned to his other work and let the file recede slightly — not closed, but no longer active. The day-to-day demands of practice asserted themselves, as they always did. Deadlines were met. Advice was given. Other questions were answered.

Still, from time to time, another message would arrive — copied, forwarded, informational — each one confirming that the work was continuing in his absence.

The matter was not finished.

But it was continuing without him.

Timing

The change was small enough that Buckland almost missed it.

He noticed it only because he had been expecting something else.

The transaction timetable had been circulating in draft for weeks, revised and refined but never substantially altered. Dates moved slightly, as they always did, but the sequence remained intact. When the latest version arrived, Buckland opened it with the casual attention he reserved for documents that had already declared their intentions.

He read it once, then again.

One line had changed.

The milestone itself was the same, the description unaltered. Only the timing had shifted. What had been scheduled for early in the month now sat under a heading marked TBC, with a note beneath it indicating that confirmation was pending "further internal alignment."

There was no reference to him. No citation. No explanation.

Buckland closed the document and set it aside.

Later that afternoon, a short message arrived from an intermediary he recognised from earlier correspondence.

We're just taking a little more time on this internally. Nothing substantive — purely procedural.

Buckland read the sentence carefully.

Purely procedural was a phrase people used when they did not yet want to say what had changed, or when they did not know how to describe it themselves.

He replied with a brief acknowledgment and returned to his work.

Over the next few days, similar signals appeared. A draft communication that had once spoken confidently of completion now referred instead to anticipated progress. A reference to external comfort was softened into a reference to continued engagement. None of the changes altered the substance of what was proposed.

They altered only the tone.

Buckland began to recognise the pattern. No one was withdrawing. No one was objecting. No one was invoking his opinion directly.

They were simply allowing more time.

That, he knew, was how confidence registered its first doubts.

By the end of the week, the original file had not moved closer to resolution. It had not moved away from it either. It sat in a kind of procedural suspension, its edges intact, its centre undisturbed.

The matter was continuing without him.

And now, elsewhere, it was hesitating.

Closure

Buckland finished the day's work earlier than he had expected.

There was nothing urgent left to do that evening, nothing that could not wait until morning.

He closed the last file and shut down the computer.

The office was quiet in the particular way it became at the end of a working day, when the house around it had resumed its ordinary life. He stood for a moment by the window, not looking for anything in particular, and then reached for the light.

Before leaving, he returned to the cabinet and removed the file from the original matter. He did not open it. He checked the label, confirmed its place in sequence, and returned it to the shelf.

The action was deliberate, but not ceremonial.

The matter was closed.

The assumptions it rested on remained.

That distinction no longer troubled him. Not because it had ceased to matter, but because he now understood how such distinctions were carried forward, redistributed, and absorbed into the machinery of ordinary practice.

He shut the cabinet and took his coat from the back of the chair.

Tomorrow, he would continue with the new work. He would be precise, as he always was. He would say no more than the framework required, and no less than it allowed.

Others would rely on what he wrote in ways he would not control.

That, too, was part of the work.

As he turned off the light and closed the door behind him, there was no sense of conclusion, only alignment.

For now, it was acceptable.

The street outside was already dark.

Part II After the Report

Acceptance

The acknowledgement arrived three days after the report had been issued. It was brief, correctly addressed, and expressed thanks without enthusiasm. There was no commentary on the substance, no request for clarification, and no indication that anything further would be required. Buckland read it once, noted the reference number, and filed it.

The matter had already been archived. That, too, was routine. The file contained nothing extraneous: correspondence, working papers, the final report, and the internal checklist, completed and signed. He did not reopen it. There was no reason to. The work had been delivered within scope, reviewed, and accepted. Whatever followed from it lay elsewhere.

The following days passed without incident. He answered correspondence, made a small amendment to a draft prepared earlier in the week, and returned two signed letters by email. None of it bore any relation to the closed matter. He did not expect it to.

On Thursday, a new instruction arrived. It was straightforward, the facts uncontentious, the scope clearly defined. Buckland read it carefully—not because it presented any difficulty, but because he always did. He entered the matter into his system, noted the deadlines, and acknowledged receipt. The wording was standard.

There was nothing in the instruction that recalled the earlier work. He did not look for such a connection. Professional life did not proceed by analogy. Each engagement stood on its own terms, and drawing lines between them was, at best, a private habit.

Late in the afternoon, he checked the storage cupboard where archived files were kept and noticed that one box had been mislabelled. It was a minor error. He corrected the reference number with a pen and returned the box to its place. The task took less than a minute.

That evening, he reviewed the next day's schedule and adjusted it slightly to accommodate a call that had been brought forward. He ate, read, and went to bed. Nothing about the day lingered.

If asked, he would have said that the previous matter was finished. Not merely concluded, but complete. There were no outstanding questions, no unresolved points of interpretation. The report said what it was meant to say, in language appropriate to its purpose. It had neither exceeded its brief nor fallen short of it. That was, in his view, the only standard that mattered.

The system depended on such finality. Without it, no conclusion would ever hold. Responsibility, once properly discharged, had to end somewhere.

The next morning, he began work on the new instruction.

Method

The new instruction settled quickly into place. Its parameters were ordinary enough that Buckland did not need to annotate them beyond the essentials. He extracted the relevant dates, confirmed the jurisdiction, and assembled the initial materials in the order he preferred. The work did not resist him. Most work did not.

He began, as he always did, by restating the question in neutral terms. It was a habit formed early and never abandoned. Precision at the outset spared explanation later. He made no allowance for how the answer might be received. That lay beyond his remit. His task was to arrive at a position that could be defended, using the materials properly before him, and to express it in language that admitted no excess.

He worked in measured intervals, pausing only to verify a reference or check a source he already knew would support the proposition. Nothing in the process invited reflection. There were no ambiguities worth lingering over, no thresholds that demanded judgment beyond the technical. The matter progressed exactly as it should have.

At one point, he noticed that a source document used a term loosely, as if precision were optional. Buckland corrected for it silently. He did not comment on the looseness itself. The correction was enough. The final formulation would be tighter than the materials that supported it. That was common. It was part of the service.

Midway through the afternoon, he paused to review what he had done so far. The structure held. Each step followed from the last without strain. He did not feel any satisfaction in this; satisfaction was not a useful metric. The absence of difficulty was confirmation enough.

He closed the document and left it untouched for the remainder of the day. Experience had taught him that clarity benefited from distance. What appeared complete too quickly often was not. He preferred to return to work when it had had time to become ordinary again.

The next morning, he resumed without material alteration. A single paragraph required adjustment, not because it was incorrect, but because it could be read in more than one way. He tightened it until the alternative reading collapsed. The revision did not change the conclusion. It merely reduced the number of places where misunderstanding could take hold.

When he was finished, he set the work aside once more. There was no urgency. The deadline was generous, and haste would add nothing. He turned instead to routine correspondence, clearing what had accumulated overnight. Most messages required no reply. Those that did were answered briefly.

Nothing further was required in relation to the new instruction at that stage.

By the end of the week, the work had assumed the familiar shape of something nearing completion.

Independence

The material arrived as an enclosure, not the substance of the communication itself. Buckland noticed it only because he made a practice of checking what others treated as ancillary. The covering email was routine; its purpose limited to confirming receipt of something already expected. He read it, registered that no reply was required, and turned to the attachment.

It was not addressed to him. That, too, was unremarkable. Documents circulated. They were copied, forwarded, appended. Their relevance was often assumed rather than stated. Buckland did not object to this. He preferred to determine relevance for himself.

The enclosure was brief. It set out a position taken for a different purpose, using language that was familiar without being identical to his own. It was not his work, nor had it been prepared for him. He read it once without marking it, then again more slowly. Nothing in it was inaccurate. Nothing in it contradicted anything he had written. If anything, it was consistent — perhaps more so than he would have expected.

He did not read it as an extension of his work. That would have been a category error. It belonged to a different process, governed by different constraints. The fact that it drew on similar material did not alter that.

Parallel uses of the same facts were common. They did not imply coordination.

One passage gave him pause, not because it was wrong, but because it rested on a formulation he recognised. The wording was not identical, but the structure was unmistakable. He could see how it had been derived, and from where. The derivation was logical. He had no grounds to dispute it.

He did not annotate the passage. There was nothing to note. The enclosure had not been sent for comment, and, offering one would have been inappropriate. He closed the document and returned it to its place among the other materials relating to the current instruction.

The remainder of the day proceeded without incident. He completed a small task that had been set aside earlier in the week, responded to two enquiries, and reviewed a draft schedule for the days ahead. None of it was affected by the document he had read.

Later, as he was preparing to shut down for the evening, he considered whether the enclosure required any further attention. The answer was no. It did not fall within the scope of his current work, nor did it reopen anything that had been closed. Its relevance, such as it was, belonged elsewhere.

He archived the email and its attachment together, ensuring the reference was correct. Then he moved on.

Dependence

The recognition did not arrive all at once. It emerged gradually, without drama, as the result of ordinary comparison. Buckland did not set out to revisit the enclosure. He encountered it again only because the materials for the current instruction required him to traverse similar ground.

The resemblance was not verbal. It lay deeper than phrasing. The structure of the reasoning followed a familiar path; one he could trace without effort. The sequence was sound. Each step proceeded from the last in a way that would have satisfied him if he had been the one setting it out.

That was the difficulty.

He understood now that the enclosure was not merely consistent with his earlier work. It depended on it. Not formally, and not by reference, but in the way conclusions, once expressed, become available to other processes. The position taken elsewhere had not been improvised. It had been assembled carefully, using materials that had already been arranged.

This did not trouble him in the way error would have done. Nothing had been misused. The reasoning remained defensible at every point. The enclosure did not claim more than it was entitled to claim, nor did it attribute its certainty to anything other than the facts before it. If he had been asked to assess it on its own terms, he would have found little to criticise.

What he recognised instead was the efficiency of the transfer.

The work he had completed earlier had done exactly what it was meant to do. It had clarified, stabilised, and closed a question within the limits set for it. In doing so, it had left behind a formulation that could be lifted without distortion. The enclosure had not distorted it. That was precisely the point.

He considered, briefly, whether the enclosure imposed any obligation on him. It did not. He had not been consulted, and consultation would have been inappropriate. The matter to which it related was not his. It lay outside the scope of his current instruction and beyond the reach of the work he had already completed.

Nor did the recognition require him to revisit what he had written. There was nothing to amend. The language had been careful. The limitations were present. Anyone reading closely would have understood them. If others chose to rely on the formulation without attending to its context, that was not something he could regulate.

He set the enclosure aside again, this time without hesitation.

What remained with him was not concern, but clarity. He could see how easily the same pattern might recur, not because of any flaw in the process, but because of its success. Properly framed conclusions travelled well. That was why they were commissioned in the first place.

The realisation did not alter his work on the current instruction. He continued as before, applying the same discipline, the same restraint. Nothing in the method invited adjustment.

By the end of the day, the enclosure had been absorbed into the general mass of completed material. It had no special status. It required no response. It had simply demonstrated, with unusual neatness, how finality behaved once it left his hands.

Finality

Once the recognition had settled, Buckland examined it in the only way that mattered: procedurally.

He did not frame it as a problem. Problems demanded response. This did not. It was, instead, a condition arising after the fact, and conditions of that kind were governed less by impulse than by boundary.

The first boundary was scope. The enclosure did not fall within the terms of his current instruction. It had not been submitted for review, nor had any opinion been sought in relation to it. To treat it as though it had would be to invent a mandate after the event. That was not diligence; it was interference.

The second boundary was finality. The earlier matter had been concluded, not provisionally but definitively. The report had been issued, acknowledged, and relied upon. Reopening it in the absence of error would not strengthen its authority. It would weaken it. Professional conclusions could not be retrofitted with unease without becoming something else entirely.

He considered whether clarification might be offered, informally. The idea did not survive inspection. Clarification presupposed ambiguity. There had been none. The language had been careful, the limitations

explicit. To re-enter the discussion now would imply
that the original formulation had been inadequate,
which it had not been.

Nor was there any basis for warning. Warnings were
appropriate where risk could be mitigated or harm
prevented. Here, nothing unlawful had occurred, and
nothing improper was unfolding. The enclosure did not
misstate the position. It merely used it efficiently. To
issue a warning in such circumstances would be to
substitute personal discomfort for professional
judgment.

He turned briefly to the question of disclosure. There
was nothing to disclose. He possessed no information
that had not already been made available through
proper channels. The enclosure had not revealed a
concealed fact; it had demonstrated a consequence.
Consequences, however unwelcome, were not
themselves reportable.

Each avenue closed cleanly.

What remained was the temptation to do something
simply to relieve the pressure of understanding.
Buckland recognised that temptation for what it was.
Action taken for that reason alone would be self-
indulgent. It would serve no client, correct no error, and
uphold no principle beyond the appearance of
responsiveness.

The discipline required here was the same discipline that governed his work more generally: restraint where restraint was due.

He returned to the current instruction and completed a further section of the draft. The work advanced without difficulty. Nothing in it was altered by what he now understood. The same standards applied. The same care was taken. There was no technical reason to proceed differently.

By the time he stopped for the evening, the enclosure no longer presented itself as an unresolved matter. It had been classified, not as an issue requiring resolution, but as a demonstration of how resolution behaved once achieved.

There was nothing further to be done.

Continuation

The days that followed were unremarkable. Work continued, arrived, and concluded in the usual way. Buckland did not measure time against what he now understood. He had no reason to. Understanding was not a unit of work, and it did not alter the order in which tasks presented themselves.

He completed the current instruction within the agreed timeframe. The final draft required little adjustment. What changes were made concerned clarity rather than substance. When he was satisfied that the language admitted no excess, he issued it and recorded the date. The acknowledgement arrived later, as expected. He filed it without rereading.

Nothing further was heard in relation to the enclosure. He had not expected to hear anything. It had taken its place among other completed materials, no more prominent than the rest. If it continued to operate elsewhere, it did so beyond his sight.

One afternoon, while reviewing a separate matter, he found himself returning to a formulation he had used before. It was sound. He saw no reason to alter it. The conditions were comparable, the facts aligned, and the language remained fit for purpose. He employed it again, making only the adjustments required by context.

There was no sense of repetition in this. Consistency was not duplication. It was the mark of work that had been done properly the first time.

At the end of the week, he archived another file. The process was familiar: references checked, documents ordered, the record closed. He took no particular notice of it. Files accumulated and receded. That was their nature.

What remained was not doubt, but awareness. He understood now how little control attended the moment when work left his hands, and how much depended on the care taken before it did. That understanding did not invite remedy. It simply clarified the boundary.

He did not resist that boundary. Nor did he attempt to soften it. The standards he worked to were not instruments of comfort. They were instruments of reliability. Once applied correctly, they asked nothing further of him.

The following Monday, a new instruction arrived. He read it, noted its scope, and began.

Late to the Party

Intestate

The call came just after six.

Margaret was in the kitchen, rinsing a mug she had not finished. She let the phone ring twice before answering, more out of habit than reluctance. Numbers at that hour were rarely casual.

"Yes," she said.

There was a pause, the faint sound of movement behind the voice. The man introduced himself and waited, as though allowing the words to settle.

Her husband had been found that morning.

The rest arrived in fragments. Ambulance. No signs of distress. Nothing to suggest he had known it was coming. He had been alone, which was normal. He had been doing nothing remarkable.

Margaret thanked the man because it seemed expected. When the call ended, she remained where she was—one hand resting on the sink, the other still holding the phone. The mug tipped and fell. The sound did not register.

Andrew arrived before nine. Claire followed shortly after, carrying a bag she had picked up without thinking. The house filled with small, practical movements. Lights were turned on. Windows opened. Someone put the kettle on again.

They spoke in half-sentences, careful not to speak at the same time.

"He was fine yesterday," Andrew said.

Claire nodded. "He sounded normal."

Margaret sat at the table and watched them move. It occurred to her, with a detached clarity, that the house felt larger than it had the night before. As if something had been removed that had been holding it together.

Later, someone asked about paperwork.

It was not indelicate. It was simply necessary.

"He didn't leave a will," Margaret said. She had checked. She had been certain there was one, though she had never known where it was. Now she knew there was not.

Andrew frowned. "Are you sure?"

"Yes."

Claire sat down. "What does that mean?"

Margaret did not answer immediately. She did not know. She knew only that it complicated things she had assumed were already settled.

The funeral arrangements were straightforward. He had never liked fuss. The service was brief, attended by people from the business and a smaller number from outside it. Men shook Andrew's hand and spoke of continuity. Claire noticed the word repeated, as though repetition might make it true.

Afterwards, the business intruded.

The bank called. Suppliers followed. Staff asked questions that could not yet be answered. The office manager wanted to know who could authorise payments. Someone else asked about the lease. Another about insurance.

Margaret listened. She made notes. She told herself she would organise them later.

Andrew went to the premises the following morning. He walked through the workshop and felt, for the first time, how much of it had been arranged around one person's habits. Tools were where his father had left them. Decisions were embedded in the placement of things.

Claire came with him the next day. She stayed less than an hour.

"He ran it in his head," she said as they left. "That's the problem."

Andrew said nothing.

By the end of the week, the question they had avoided began to take shape.

What, exactly, had he left them?

The business was still trading. Orders were filled. Accounts were paid. Nothing had stopped. But nothing had moved either.

One afternoon, Margaret sat at the dining table and spread out what she had found. Bank statements. Correspondence. A thin file marked Loan. There were signatures she recognised—hers among them—but the words around them refused to arrange themselves into anything she could hold.

Andrew stood over her shoulder. "It's not that complicated," he said, without conviction.

Claire watched from the doorway. "It is if we don't know where the edges are."

Margaret looked up. "What edges?"

"The ones you fall off," Claire said.

They argued then, briefly and without heat. Andrew wanted to keep things going, at least until they knew more. Claire wanted to sell while the business still appeared intact. Margaret said little, but when she spoke, she returned to the same point.

"He worked too hard for this to just disappear."

Andrew nodded. "Exactly."

Claire looked away.

On the Friday, a letter arrived from the bank. It was polite. It expressed condolence. It requested confirmation of authority. It did not threaten anything. It did not need to.

Margaret read it twice and placed it on the table with the others.

"We need help," she said.

Andrew looked at her. "Who from?"

She hesitated. The answer was not obvious. The business had always been his domain. Decisions had been made without committees. There was no one to defer to now.

"Someone independent," Claire said. "Someone who can tell us what this actually is."

Andrew considered that. "And how much that will cost us?"

Margaret folded the letter and returned it to its envelope. "We can't decide anything without understanding it."

The room was quiet. Somewhere nearby, a lawnmower started.

For the moment, the business continued—without reference to the man who had built it or the family now responsible for it. What it would become depended on decisions they had not yet made, about obligations they did not yet understand.

Margaret gathered the papers into a single pile and aligned the edges carefully.

"We'll find someone," she said.

It was not a promise. It was a necessity.

Without Him

By Monday, the house had begun to feel provisional.

Margaret moved through it with a notebook in her hand, recording things she had never needed to write down before. Passwords she did not know. Accounts she could not identify. Names that recurred without explanation.

The business intruded by way of questions.

The office manager rang first. Her voice was steady, professional, carefully neutral.

"I just need to know who I should be taking instruction from," she said.

Margaret hesitated. "For now," she said, "from me."

There was a pause at the other end of the line—brief, but perceptible.

"Of course," the woman said. "And for authorisations?"

Margaret wrote the word down and underlined it. "We'll come to that," she said.

Andrew spent most of the day at the premises. He walked the floor, spoke to staff, reassured where he could. He knew enough to sound confident, and enough to know he was improvising.

People deferred to him because he was there.

He recognised, with some discomfort, that this was not the same thing as authority.

Claire did not go in. She worked from home, fielding calls Andrew forwarded to her. Suppliers wanted reassurance. The landlord wanted clarity. The bank wanted names.

She made lists but crossed nothing off.

That afternoon, the three of them sat at the dining table again. The papers were neater now, arranged into piles that suggested order without quite achieving it.

"It's running," Andrew said. "For the moment."

"For how long?" Claire asked.

Andrew shrugged. "Long enough to work something out."

Margaret looked at the notebook in front of her. "Your father used to decide these things without telling anyone," she said. "Now we have to decide them without knowing how he did."

Claire said, "That's the problem."

They fell quiet.

Later, Margaret returned to the thin loan file. The figures were clear enough. What they represented was not. She recognised her signature in several places. She did not remember signing most of them.

Andrew stood behind her. "It's just paperwork," he said.

She did not look up. "It's never just paperwork."

The phone rang again. This time it was the bank, following up on the letter.

"We'll need confirmation of signing authority," the man said. "In writing."

Margaret thanked him and ended the call.

Claire closed her laptop. "They're not waiting for us," she said.

"No," Margaret replied. "They're waiting for certainty."

Andrew pushed his chair back. "So, what do we do?"

Margaret considered the question carefully before answering. "We find out what this actually is," she said. "Before it tells us."

Andrew frowned. "How?"

Claire looked at him. "From someone who isn't invested in what we want it to be."

The answer settled between them—not yet a plan, but no longer a thought.

Without him, the business was still moving. Orders were filled. Wages were paid. Nothing had failed.

But everything that mattered now required a decision.

And no one was certain who, exactly, was entitled to make it.

Positions

By midweek, the arrangements had settled into a pattern.

Not a comfortable one, but a workable one. Phones were answered. Emails were returned. The business continued to present problems in the same way it always had—incrementally, without regard for timing.

Andrew began each morning at the premises. He arrived early, left late, and learned quickly which questions could be deferred and which could not. Staff accepted his presence without enthusiasm or resistance. He was, after all, the son.

What unsettled him was how often he was asked to decide things he did not yet understand.

Claire took a different approach. She stayed out of the building unless she had to be there. Distance, she found, helped her see the shape of things. She reviewed contracts sent through by the office manager, flagged what she could not follow, and asked questions that were rarely answered fully.

"You're thinking about this like it's already over," Andrew said to her one evening.

"I'm thinking about it like it might be," Claire replied.

Margaret listened to them both.

She spent most of her time with the papers. Not in any systematic way—she lacked the language for that—but with a growing sense of unease. There were accounts she did not recognise and obligations she had assumed were long resolved. She kept finding her own signature in places she did not remember signing.

That troubled her more than anything else.

They spoke about the future in the abstract.

Andrew talked about potential. The business had room to grow. His father had always been conservative, reluctant to borrow beyond what was necessary. There were efficiencies to be found, markets he had never pursued.

"He was careful," Andrew said. "That doesn't mean he was right."

Claire was unmoved. "Careful kept it alive."

Margaret said nothing, but when they spoke of selling, she stiffened.

"He worked too hard for that," she said. "Too long."

Andrew nodded. Claire did not.

"What matters," Claire said, "is what it's actually worth. Not what it cost him."

The words hung between them, factual and unwelcome.

Later that night, Margaret returned to the loan file again. She read it slowly, line by line. The numbers made sense. The terms did not. She began to understand that the business was not a single thing, but an accumulation of arrangements layered over time.

None of them had been designed to be examined all at once.

When she mentioned this the next morning, Andrew waved it away. "Every business looks messy when you pull it apart."

"That's not what I mean," she said. "I don't know where it ends."

Claire looked up from her laptop. "That's the part we need to know."

They argued again, briefly. Andrew accused Claire of being impatient. Claire accused Andrew of being sentimental. Margaret ended it by asking them both to stop.

"We're talking past each other," she said. "And we don't know enough yet."

Andrew sighed. "So, what do you want to do?"

Margaret did not answer immediately. She had learned, over the years, that the first answer was rarely the right one.

"I want to understand what obligations we've inherited," she said at last. "All of them."

"And then?" Andrew asked.

"Then we decide what's possible," she said. "Not what we'd like."

Claire closed her laptop. "That means getting outside help."

Andrew grimaced. "That means cost."

"Yes," Margaret said. "But ignorance costs more."

The room fell quiet.

They had not reached agreement. They had, however, reached the edge of what they could do on their own.

Whatever happened next would depend on someone who did not belong to the family—and was not invested in preserving any of their assumptions.

An Introduction

They did not decide immediately.

There were practicalities to attend to first— signatures to chase, calls to return, forms to complete that asked questions none of them could yet answer with confidence. The business continued to demand attention in small, insistent ways, leaving little space for reflection.

It was Claire who raised the subject again.

"I spoke to the office manager," she said one evening. "She asked if we were bringing anyone in."

Andrew looked up. "Anyone?"

"An accountant. An adviser. Someone who isn't us."

Margaret was quiet for a moment. "Did she suggest anyone?"

"She said your father dealt with a forensic auditor years ago," Claire replied. "Not for this. Through a larger matter."

Andrew frowned. "Forensic sounds expensive."

"It also sounds like someone who looks at what's there, not what they hope is there," Claire said.

Margaret considered that. Her husband had rarely spoken about outside advisers. When he had, it was usually to complain about them.

"What's his name?" she asked.

Claire checked her phone. "John Buckland."

Andrew repeated it, as if testing whether it meant anything to him. It did not.

Margaret said, "Did she say what he did?"

"She said he was thorough," Claire replied. "And that dad respected his work."

That gave Margaret pause. Her husband had been selective about who he relied upon.

They did not call immediately. Andrew wanted to think about scope. Claire wanted to know fees. Margaret wanted to be sure they were not inviting someone in who would tell them only what they already knew.

The decision came the following morning, prompted by nothing more dramatic than another letter from the bank.

Margaret read it, folded it carefully, and placed it with the others.

"We'll speak to him," she said. "At least hear what he says."

Claire nodded. Andrew hesitated, then agreed.

The call was brief.

John Buckland answered himself. His voice was neutral, unhurried.

Margaret explained the situation as clearly as she could. Death. No will. A small business. Uncertainty.

He listened without interruption.

When she finished, there was a pause—not hesitation, but consideration.

"I can meet," he said. "To understand the position."

"And after that?" Margaret asked.

"We'll see," he replied. "I don't know enough yet to suggest more."

They arranged a time.

When the call ended Margaret relayed the gist of the conversation to the others. Andrew raised an eyebrow at Claire. Margaret found that she liked the answer.

There was no sense of relief, only a shift. Something had been set in motion that seemed like progress.

Andrew said, "He didn't promise anything."

"No," Margaret said. "He didn't."

Claire closed her notebook. "That's probably a good sign."

Margaret gathered the papers from the table and stacked them neatly. For the first time since her husband's death, she felt they were no longer circling the same questions.

They were about to hand them to someone who would insist on better ones.

Terms of Engagement

John arrived ten minutes early and waited in the car.

It was a habit he had never entirely shaken. Arriving early allowed the room to settle before he entered. Arriving late allowed others to claim the shape of the meeting. He preferred neither. When the minute hand touched the hour, he switched off the engine, gathered his folder, and walked to the door.

Margaret answered it herself, composed and businesslike. "Mr Buckland?" she said. "Thank you for coming."

Inside, the house retained the faint orderliness of a life that had been interrupted rather than concluded. There were no signs of mourning beyond the absence itself. The dining table had been cleared and extended, three chairs drawn back. A fourth stood at the head, unoccupied.

Andrew rose as John entered. He was late thirties, perhaps—and wore the confidence of someone accustomed to speaking before knowing whether it was necessary. Claire remained seated, arms folded loosely, watching John with a polite attentiveness that did not yet extend to trust.

They exchanged names. John declined the offer of tea.

Margaret gestured to the empty chair at the head of the table. "We thought it might be easier if you explained—well—what it is you actually do."

John placed his folder on the table but did not open it.

"That depends," he said, "on what you want to know."

Andrew smiled. "We want to know whether the business is sound."

John inclined his head. "Sound can mean several things."

Claire said, "We want to know whether it's worth continuing."

John turned slightly toward her. "Worth to whom?"

A brief silence followed. It was not hostile, merely unaccustomed.

Margaret spoke first. "My husband worked on it for over twenty years," she said. "I don't want us to discover too late that we've misunderstood something important."

John nodded. He had heard that sentence in many forms. It was usually sincere.

"I can review the financial records," he said. "I can tell you how the business has been performing, what obligations it carries, and what risks attach to different courses of action. I can't tell you what decision to make."

Andrew leaned forward. "We're not asking you to decide for us. We just need the facts."

John allowed a small pause. "Facts," he said, "arrive in stages."

He opened the folder and slid a single page toward the centre of the table.

"This would be an initial engagement," he said. "Limited in scope. I would review the accounts as they stand, assess liquidity, debt, and operational viability. I would also look at governance—who can act, who cannot, and where authority currently rests."

Claire glanced down at the page. "And after that?"

"After that," John said, "you may decide you've learned enough. Or you may decide you want me to look further. That would be a separate instruction."

Andrew scanned the page quickly. "This doesn't include valuation."

"No," John said.

"Why not?"

"Valuation answers a different question," John said. "And it relies on assumptions you haven't agreed yet."

Andrew frowned. "It would be useful to know what it's worth."

John met his gaze without challenge. "It would be premature."

Claire leaned back, folding her arms across her chest.

John folded his hands and let them rest on the table. "I work in phases," he said. "Each phase answers a defined question. Each phase has a cost."

Margaret asked, "Can you give us an idea?"

"Yes," John said. "I can give you a range."

He named it. He did not qualify it.

Andrew's eyebrows lifted. Claire's mouth tightened almost imperceptibly.

"That's just for the first stage?" Claire asked.

"Yes."

"And if we want more?"

"Then there is more."

Andrew laughed lightly. "You don't mince words."

"I try not to," John said. "It avoids misunderstanding."

Margaret studied the page again. "And if we decide to stop after this?"

"Then you stop," John said. "I provide what I've found to that point. No conclusions beyond the scope."

Andrew tapped the table with a finger. "Seems cautious."

"It is," John said. "Caution is cheaper than correction."

Claire said, "Or more expensive."

John turned to her. "Only if you continue."

The air in the room shifted slightly—not tension, but consideration.

Andrew said, "We're not a large operation. This isn't—corporate."

John acknowledged the point. "Which is why I'm suggesting a limited review. Corporate engagements tend to assume continuation. Yours does not."

Margaret looked from one child to the other. "We need to know where we stand."

Claire said, "We need to know how much this is going to cost us."

Andrew said, "We need to know whether it's worth spending anything at all."

John waited. Silence, used sparingly, was often the most effective instrument available.

At last, Margaret said, "If we do nothing, what happens?"

John answered carefully. "The business continues to exist. Obligations continue to accrue. Decisions will still be made—by default rather than intention."

Andrew leaned back. "So doing nothing isn't free."

"No," John said. "It is simply unpriced."

Claire sighed. "I don't like open-ended arrangements."

"Nor do I," John said. "That's why I stop when the brief ends."

Andrew glanced at his mother. "I think we should do it. At least the first stage."

Claire said, "I think we should be careful this doesn't turn into a fishing expedition."

John met her eye. "I don't fish," he said. "I examine what's put before me. If something suggests itself, I'll tell you. You decide whether to proceed—or not."

Margaret reached for a pen. "We should begin," she said. "I don't want to look back and think we avoided knowing."

Claire watched her sign. Andrew nodded, satisfied.

John took the page back, folded it once, and placed it in his folder.

"I'll need access to the accounts," he said. "Bank correspondence. Loan documents. Anything relating to ownership or guarantees."

Andrew waved a hand. "That's all straightforward."

John did not comment.

"I'll invoice at the end of the phase," he said. "If at any point you wish me to stop, tell me. I will stop."

Claire said, "And if we ask you to continue?"

"Then I will tell you what it will cost," John said. "Before I do the work."

Margaret looked relieved, as though a structure had been erected around something that had previously felt amorphous.

John stood. "I'll be in touch once I've reviewed the initial material."

As he left, he felt the familiar sensation settle—not anticipation, but alignment. The work had boundaries. The boundaries would be tested. They always were.

In the car, he made a single note before starting the engine.

Family agreed to limited scope. Cost already a point of tension. Expect resistance if implications widen.

He closed the pad, drove away, and left the house to its deliberations.

Authority

John sent the detailed engagement letter that afternoon.

He kept it brief. Scope, timing, fee range. No commentary. No assurances. The language was deliberately unadorned. He had learned that documents which tried to persuade tended to outlive their usefulness.

The reply came the following morning. Margaret's name appeared alone on the email.

We are agreed to proceed on the basis you outlined. Please let us know what you require first.

John read it once, then again. There were no conditions attached, no requests for reassurance. That, too, told him something.

He replied with a list.

Bank statements. Loan agreements. Supplier contracts. Payroll summaries. Any correspondence relating to ownership or guarantees.

He did not explain why.

Two days later, the boxes arrived.

Margaret delivered them herself, carrying one and leaving the others in the boot for John to retrieve.

"I don't expect you to find anything," she said as they stood at the edge of the drive. "But I don't want us guessing."

"That's sensible," John said.

She hesitated. "Andrew thinks this is unnecessary."

John nodded. "He may be right."

That surprised her. "You think so?"

"I don't know yet," John said. "That's the point."

She smiled faintly at that, then grew serious again. "And if it turns out not to be?"

"Then you'll know where you stand," John said.

She considered this. "That matters."

"It usually does," John said.

Inside, John signed the acknowledgment of receipt and placed it on top of the box. He did not open anything. Not yet.

Margaret lingered in the doorway. "How long will it take?"

"Long enough," John said. "Not longer."

When she had gone, John carried the boxes to his study and placed them beside the desk. He washed his hands first, dried them carefully, and returned to the room.

He sat, adjusted the chair, and opened the first box.

The work had begun.

Orderly Books

John worked through the first box methodically.

There was nothing haphazard about the records. Invoices were filed by month, bank statements reconciled without flourish, payroll summaries consistent. Expenses appeared where they should. Income was recorded without optimism. Nothing strained toward concealment.

He noted it and moved on.

By mid-morning he had confirmed the obvious: the business was not careless. Whatever else it might be, it was not sloppy. He made a brief note to that effect and closed the ledger.

The second box told the same story. Depreciation schedules were conservative. Asset values were understated rather than indulged. There were no last-minute adjustments clustered around reporting dates, no hurried reclassifications to improve appearance.

It did not appear that anybody had tried to make the numbers look better than they were.

John paused, reread a page, then set it aside. He did not linger. Competence, once established, rarely repaid further attention.

In the afternoon he turned to the slim folder marked Bank. It contained correspondence rather than statements—letters, emails, confirmations. The tone was courteous, almost familiar. Requests were answered promptly. Extensions, where granted, were recorded without fuss.

He made another note.

Relationship predates need.

It was not a conclusion. Just an observation.

By the end of the day, John had a provisional view. The business was modest, stable, and dependent. Its margins were narrow but predictable. It required judgment more than ingenuity.

That judgment had belonged to one man.

John closed the folder and stacked the boxes neatly. He had not yet seen anything that justified alarm. He had also not seen anything that explained continuity in the absence of its founder.

Both absences mattered.

He stood, stretched his back, and left the room. He did not review his notes again that evening. There would be time for that later.

Orderly books had a way of encouraging premature confidence. He preferred to let that settle before testing it.

A Provisional View

John returned to his notes the following morning.

He read them in sequence, then out of order. The habit was not superstition; patterns revealed themselves differently when chronology was disrupted. This time, nothing resisted.

The business was modest and tightly run. Cash flow was narrow but predictable. There were no unexplained movements, no sudden compressions or expansions that suggested strain. Inventory turned as expected. Staff costs were stable. The margins left little room for error, but they had not been eroded by indulgence.

John wrote a single word at the top of the page: Viable.

He underlined it twice.

What the figures did not show was equally important. There was no capacity for absence. The founder's judgment had not been replaced by process; it had been embedded. Decisions that might once have been routine now lacked a point of reference.

This was not unusual. Many small businesses functioned this way. They survived on familiarity and habit, neither of which transferred easily.

By late morning, John had reached the limit of what the initial scope would support. He had an answer to the question he had been asked, though it was narrower than the family might expect.

He drafted a short summary.

The business is solvent and conservatively reported. It is operationally dependent on its founder's involvement. Continuation without structural change carries increased risk.

He saved the document without embellishment.

In the afternoon, he turned briefly to the matter of valuation, then set it aside. Any number he produced now would carry false authority. Value assumed continuity. Continuity had not yet been established.

John closed the file.

The work so far suggested a business that could continue, provided decisions were made promptly and competently. It did not suggest one that could absorb indecision.

He was aware, even as he reached that conclusion, that it rested on absence: no irregularities, no misstatements, no immediate exposures. Absence was a poor foundation for confidence, but it was often the only one available at first pass.

John leaned back and looked at the window, considering whether anything he had seen justified expanding the scope. On the face of it, nothing did. That, too, was information.

He left the desk and did not return to it until evening. When he did, he added a final note beneath the others.

Assessment provisional. Dependent on completeness of view.

He closed the folder.

Provisional conclusions had a way of settling too comfortably if left unchallenged. John had learned not to trust them for long.

Pressure to Conclude

John sent the summary the following morning.

He kept the email as spare as the document it attached. No framing, no reassurance. He had learned that conclusions travelled better when they were allowed to arrive without escort.

The reply came first from Claire.

Thank you. If the business is viable, we should probably move toward a valuation.

John read it once and set it aside.

Andrew's response followed an hour later.

This is encouraging. I'd like to talk about next steps—growth potential, not just continuity.

Margaret did not write.

That afternoon, John returned to the house at their request. The dining table had been cleared again, the same chairs drawn back. The fourth was no longer empty.

Claire spoke first. "We've read your summary."

John nodded.

"It sounds," she continued, "as though there's nothing fundamentally wrong."

"There is nothing immediately visible," John said.

Andrew smiled. "That's what we needed to hear."

John did not respond.

"So," Claire said, "the question becomes how much further we need to go. We don't want to spend money proving what already seems clear."

John folded his hands. "What seems clear is limited to what I've reviewed."

Andrew leaned forward. "But you've looked at the accounts. The bank's happy. Suppliers are paid. Staff are settled."

"Yes," John said.

"Then why keep going?"

John looked at him. "Because I was asked whether the business was viable. Not whether it was exposed."

Claire frowned. "Isn't that the same thing?"

"Not always."

Margaret shifted slightly in her chair. "Can you explain?"

John chose his words carefully. "Viability answers whether the business can operate. Exposure answers who bears the risk when it does."

Andrew waved a hand. "Every business has risk."

"Yes," John said. "But not every risk is understood by the people carrying it."

Claire said, "You're suggesting there's something specific."

"I'm saying I don't yet know," John replied. "And that not knowing can be expensive."

She studied him. "We hired you to tell us what you know."

"And I have," John said. "Within scope."

Andrew's tone hardened. "This feels like a technical distinction."

John did not dispute it. "Many consequential ones are."

Claire tapped the summary with a finger. "If we stop here, what happens?"

"You proceed on the assumption that what you haven't examined does not matter," John said.

"And if it does?"

"Then it will assert itself later."

Margaret had been silent until now. "Are you recommending we continue?"

John shook his head. "I don't recommend. I describe."

Andrew exhaled. "You must have a view."

"I have one," John said. "It isn't complete."

Claire leaned back in her chair. She did not speak.

Margaret looked at him. "How much further would you need to go?"

John answered without hesitation. "Enough to understand how obligations attach. Beyond the business itself."

"And that costs more," Claire said.

"Yes."

Andrew stood. "We're not committing to that today."

John accepted this. "Then my work stops here."

The words settled differently this time. Not as reassurance, but as a boundary.

Margaret looked at him. "You mean—now?"

"Yes."

Claire said, "That seems abrupt."

"It's precise," John said. "I've completed what I was asked to do."

Andrew glanced at his mother. "We'll need to talk."

"Of course," John said. "Take your time."

He gathered his papers, careful not to rush. The summary that had felt reassuring that morning now seemed provisional in a different way.

At the door, Margaret said quietly, "Thank you for your honesty."

John inclined his head. "It's what you're paying for."

Outside, John paused on the path, the afternoon had turned overcast. He continued to his car.

Notification

John did not return to the accounts immediately.

Before closing the file entirely, he returned once more to the correspondence: emails, letters, confirmations—material that sat alongside the numbers without belonging to them. He had learned that what organisations said to one another often revealed more than what they recorded.

The supplier agreements were unremarkable. Terms were stable, margins thin. Relationships appeared long-standing rather than negotiated. There was an absence of churn that suggested familiarity rather than leverage.

He made a note and moved on.

The bank correspondence was more interesting.

Not because it was irregular—it was not—but because of its tone. Requests were met without delay. Extensions, where granted, were framed as routine rather than concession. There was no evidence of escalation, no invocation of policy, no sense of distance.

The language was courteous. Almost personal.

John read one email twice, then checked the date. It predated the most recent facility amendment by several years. Another followed the same pattern. The sequence mattered.

He wrote a short note in the margin.

Accommodation precedes pressure.

It was not yet a conclusion. It was a direction of travel.

He considered whether this belonged within the scope of his engagement. On paper, it did not. Correspondence tone was not a line item. But tone shaped behaviour, and behaviour shaped outcomes.

John checked the signatories on the emails. Names repeated. Titles did not.

He leaned forward and reread the thread from the beginning.

The bank had not been dealing with a structure. It had been dealing with a person.

John closed the folder and sat back. This did not contradict his provisional assessment. The business could still be viable. But viability built on familiarity was fragile when familiarity ended.

He reached for his pad and wrote another note, more cautiously this time.

Continuity assumptions implicit.

He did not underline it.

This was not yet something to raise with the family. It was adjacent to their question, not inside it. But it narrowed the margin for error.

John returned the folder to the stack and left the room.

In the kitchen, he made tea and let it cool untouched. His attention remained with the correspondence, with what had not been said as much as what had.

External signals rarely announced themselves. They accumulated, quietly, until they changed the weight of a decision.

By the time John returned to his desk, he knew one thing clearly: stopping now would be easy.

Continuing would not.

Interlude — The Bank's View

The notification arrived without ceremony.

A standard form, scanned and forwarded from a branch office, marked Deceased — Primary Contact. It did not require immediate action. The system acknowledged receipt automatically and routed the file to a queue that was reviewed twice a week.

No alert was triggered.

The account had not been in arrears. Payments were current. Facilities were within covenant. From a distance, there was nothing to distinguish it from dozens of others that passed through the same channel each month.

When the file was opened again three days later, it was not because of urgency but classification.

The relationship manager assigned to the account had already been reassigned. His name appeared in the historical notes, but the active field was blank. The system flagged this as incomplete and requested allocation.

The credit officer who picked it up did so between meetings. He skimmed the summary first, then the timeline. Twenty years of trading history compressed into a few screens. Facility extensions. Renewals. Incremental adjustments. Nothing abrupt.

He noted the length of the relationship and the absence of dispute.

That mattered.

Accounts with long histories were rarely volatile. They did not surprise. Whatever risk they carried had already declared itself, slowly, in ways that were easy to accommodate. The system treated such files as stable unless proven otherwise.

The death of the principal did not, in itself, constitute proof of increased risk.

The officer scrolled through the correspondence. The tone was familiar, almost conversational. Requests framed as updates rather than demands. Replies prompt. Extensions recorded without reference to escalation or exception.

There was no record of committee intervention.

He made a brief note.

Relationship managed at branch level. Discretion exercised.

That discretion no longer applied.

The file was reassigned formally the following week. No meeting was convened. There was no reason to convene one. The exposure was modest. The guarantees were clear. The facility sat well within tolerances.

What had changed was not the risk but the reference point.

The officer read the guarantee language carefully. Joint and several. Continuing. Not limited by variation or repayment. The wording had been carried forward intact through each amendment, reproduced without comment.

There was no ambiguity.

He opened the related entities tab and confirmed ownership. The company was unchanged. No transition provisions. No succession arrangements noted. The death had not altered the structure; it had merely removed the person through whom judgment had previously been exercised.

That was a familiar configuration.

Many small businesses operated this way. They relied on continuity of habit rather than continuity of design. As long as habit persisted, the distinction did not matter.

The system was indifferent to habit.

The officer updated the classification. Not high risk. Not distressed. Simply relationship change. That status carried procedural consequences rather than immediate action.

Correspondence would be standardised. Decisions would be documented. Discretion would be limited to what policy permitted.

He paused briefly over the guarantor details.

Spouse. No ownership interest. No management role recorded.

He checked the exposure again. It was material, but not unusual.

There was no requirement to notify the guarantor of any change. The terms were already in force. There was no breach to cure and no decision to make.

Waiting was the rational course.

He closed the file and moved on to the next item in the queue.

By the time the family made contact weeks later, the position would already have settled. Not because anyone had decided anything, but because nothing needed deciding.

The system functioned best when it did not intervene.

The file would remain open, current, and quietly inert until something forced it to move. A request. A proposal. A deviation from what had previously been routine.

Until then, the exposure would sit where it had always sat, unchanged by explanation.

The officer shut down his screen at the end of the day without giving the account further thought. There was nothing unresolved.

From the bank's perspective, nothing had yet happened.

Interlude — Andrew

Andrew arrived at the premises before anyone else.

He had begun doing this without deciding to. The habit felt inherited rather than chosen. He unlocked the door, switched on the lights, and stood for a moment, waiting for the building to respond in the way it once had. It did not.

The workshop smelled the same. Oil, dust, metal. The familiarity steadied him. He walked the floor, touching nothing, checking that everything was where it should be. It was. That, too, was unsettling.

His father had moved through the space with an ease that came from repetition. Decisions had been made in passing. A tool left out meant something. A bench cleared meant something else. Andrew tried to read those signals now, but they no longer resolved into instruction.

He opened the office door and sat at the desk. The chair felt wrong. He adjusted it, then adjusted it again.

Emails waited in the inbox. Most were routine. A supplier confirming delivery. A staff member asking about leave. He replied where he could, deferring what he could not. The act of answering steadied him. It created the impression of motion.

As others arrived. They greeted him politely, with a caution that had not been there before. He was aware of being watched, not with suspicion, but with a question he could not yet answer.

He walked the floor again, offering reassurance. He spoke confidently, because that was expected of him. The words came easily. Their effect did not.

When the adviser rang, Andrew let it go to voicemail.

He listened to the message twice. The tone was neutral, professional. A request to clarify scope. A suggestion to meet.

Andrew did not return the call.

At lunch, he ate at his desk. He stared at a set of figures he had printed earlier and tried to see them as his father would have. He could not remember ever watching him do this. The work had always appeared already done.

In the afternoon, a small decision presented itself. A piece of equipment had failed. It was not urgent, but it would become so if left unattended. Andrew authorised the repair without hesitation. It felt good to decide something that mattered.

Later, he realised the decision had been inconsequential.

The business continued to operate around him rather than through him. Processes absorbed his input without acknowledging it. The systems did not resist him, but they did not require him either.

By the end of the day, he was exhausted.

As he locked up, Andrew stood in the doorway and looked back at the space. He tried to imagine it responding to him as it had to his father. The thought made him uneasy.

He drove home without turning on the radio.

Interlude — Claire

Claire did not go to the premises.

She worked at the dining table, laptop open, papers arranged carefully to one side. The distance was deliberate. She wanted to see the situation as a set of conditions rather than a place.

She read everything she was sent. She read slowly, without urgency. Where Andrew looked for continuity, Claire looked for exit.

The documents unsettled her, not because they were alarming, but because they were orderly. The obligations were clear. The exposure was cumulative. Nothing suggested rescue.

She made notes, not of tasks, but of outcomes. If this happened, then that followed. If they waited, this increased. The logic was impersonal and difficult to dispute.

Claire spoke to her mother in the evenings. The conversations were careful. They avoided conclusions. Claire did not push. She did not reassure either.

She noticed how often Margaret said she understood.

Understanding, Claire thought, was not the same as safety.

When Andrew rang, she let the call go unanswered. Not out of avoidance, but because she did not know what she could say that would not harden into position.

She imagined the business sold and felt relief. She imagined it continuing and felt dread. Neither image brought satisfaction.

What troubled her most was the absence of an outcome that did not require someone to absorb loss. The question was not whether loss would occur, but where it would land.

Late one afternoon, she received a copy of the adviser's proposed terms. She read them once and closed the file.

This, she thought, was what clarity looked like.

She did not yet know how to persuade anyone else.

Execution

"The accounts arrived in three cardboard boxes, and a slim folder marked Bank, sent on to supplement the material already gathered."

John preferred paper when it was available. Not because it was more truthful—nothing was—but because it revealed its age and handling. Electronic records were tidy by default. Paper had habits.

He worked at the dining table in his own house, the surface cleared to the edges, the boxes arranged in order of receipt rather than relevance. Relevance declared itself later.

The business accounts were conservative. Expenses were recorded promptly, income without optimism. Depreciation schedules were dull and consistent. There was no sign of desperation—no late reclassifications, no frantic adjustments near reporting dates. If anything, the numbers erred toward caution.

John made notes sparingly.

He spent the first afternoon confirming what was there. The second identifying what was not. It was only on the third morning, with the folder open and the light angled low across the table, that the pattern began to assert itself.

The loan documents were straightforward. Original facility agreement. Amendments. Correspondence. Extensions granted quietly, without apparent negotiation. The sort of accommodation banks extended to people they trusted—or had learned not to challenge.

John read them in sequence, then again out of order.

The signatures repeated—nothing remarkable in that. Their placement was.

He separated the documents into two piles.

On one side, documents executed by the business: agreements, confirmations, covenants. On the other, documents executed personally.

The same name appeared throughout.

Margaret.

Her signature was steady. No sign of reluctance or haste. He noted the dates. Early on, close to the founding. Later, at points where the business had clearly required reassurance rather than expansion.

John retrieved the company constitution. Then the share register.

Margaret was not listed.

He checked again, slower this time.

No shares. No directorship. No recorded partnership interest.

He leaned back in his chair and allowed that to settle.

It was not uncommon. Many spouses believed themselves to be partners in all but name. Many businesses encouraged the ambiguity. What mattered was not belief but exposure.

John returned to the loan agreements. The language was precise. Joint and several. Continuing guarantee. Not limited by repayment or variation.

He marked a page with a slip of paper and moved on.

The guarantee was not extinguished by the husband's death. It could not be. It had been designed to survive exactly this sort of event.

John made another pile.

There were no signs of deceit. No forged signatures. No concealment. The documents had been there all along, executed openly, renewed as required. The misunderstanding was structural, not moral.

He checked the balance of the loan. It had reduced, but not materially. There were other obligations too— supplier agreements with personal undertakings attached, quietly renewed.

John closed the folder.

He looked at the clock. Late afternoon. Too early to call. Too important not to pause.

He wrote a short note in his pad.

Spouse is guarantor only. No ownership interest. Guarantees live. Sale does not clear exposure.

He underlined the last sentence once.

John returned the documents to their folders, carefully, exactly as he had found them. He placed them back in the box and sealed it.

Then he stopped work.

That evening, he drafted an email and deleted it. Drafted another and reduced it to three sentences.

I have identified an issue that extends beyond the scope of my current engagement. It concerns personal exposure rather than business performance. I will need written authorisation to continue.

He sent it to Margaret, copying Andrew and Claire.

He did not attach documents. He did not explain.

He closed the laptop and made himself a simple meal, eaten standing at the kitchen bench. The habit of stopping cleanly was another thing he had learned early. Continuing without authority blurred responsibility.

Later, as the light faded, his phone vibrated once. A message from Andrew.

Can you at least tell us if this is serious?

John read it and set the phone face down on the table.

Serious was a word that invited argument. Consequence was harder to dispute.

He washed the plate, dried it, and returned it to the cupboard.

On his desk, the sealed box waited, inert and patient.

John left it there.

Authorisation Resumed

The email arrived just after nine.

It was from Margaret, brief and unambiguous.

We would like you to continue. Please let us know what that entails.

John read it once and set it aside.

He did not reply immediately. Instead, he reviewed his notes from the initial phase, then the margins he had marked in the bank correspondence. Nothing had changed. What had changed was permission.

He drafted a response carefully.

Continuing will require an expanded scope. I will need to examine personal guarantees, founding documentation, and lender correspondence in full. I will confirm the additional cost before proceeding.

He sent it and closed the file.

The reply came an hour later.

Understood. Please proceed.

There was no discussion of figures. That omission was deliberate, John thought. Agreement was easier before cost was named.

He prepared the revised engagement letter and sent it over. This one was longer. Not by much, but enough. It described what had previously been peripheral as central. It made explicit what had been assumed.

Margaret signed and returned it the same afternoon.

Andrew followed later, with a separate message.

Just so we're clear, this doesn't mean we're assuming the worst.

John replied with a single sentence.

It means we are prepared to understand it.

After that, there was nothing more to say.

John reopened the box he had sealed and removed the loan documents. He read them again, slower this time, with a different question in mind. Not how healthy is the business, but who stands behind it.

The distinction sharpened everything.

He traced the sequence of signatures, the renewals that carried forward without comment, the language that assumed continuity because continuity had never been tested.

By early evening, he had confirmed what he had already suspected. The exposure was not accidental. It was structural.

John stopped for the night.

Authorisation did not oblige immediacy. It obliged care.

He closed the folder, placed it back in the drawer, and made a final note for the day.

Scope expanded. Consequences unavoidable.

The work had crossed its threshold. From here on, it would not be possible to return to reassurance without explanation.

Reconstruction

John began at the beginning.

Not with the accounts as they now stood, but with the first documents that had allowed the business to exist at all. The founding loan agreement was thin, almost modest in its ambition. The sums involved were not large. The assumptions were.

He laid the documents out in sequence across the desk and read them without haste.

The structure was simple. A company formed to trade. A facility extended on the strength of projected cash flow and personal assurance. The distinction between the two had never been tested, because it had never needed to be.

John followed the amendments forward. Each renewal carried the same language, slightly reworked, never challenged. The figures changed. The obligations did not. What had once been a short-term accommodation had become a standing arrangement.

He made a note.

Risk rolled forward, not retired.

The guarantee appeared early. It was not buried. It did not need to be. It sat where such things often did, in the section no one reread once it had been signed the first time. Margaret's name appeared beneath her husband's, steady and unqualified.

There was no reference to ownership. None was required.

John checked the correspondence that followed. Each time the facility was renewed, the language assumed continuity. The bank thanked them for their cooperation. The tone suggested mutual understanding rather than formal assessment.

This was not negligence. It was familiarity.

He turned to the supplier agreements. Most were commercial. A few were not. Two contained personal undertakings that mirrored the bank's comfort, extended on the strength of a man who was no longer there.

John paused and checked dates.

The undertakings clustered around a period of expansion—measured, not reckless. New equipment. Additional staff. Nothing extravagant. Each step justified at the time, none revisited afterward.

He drew the strands together slowly.

The business had been viable because its risks were absorbed privately. Its margins had been sufficient because exposure sat outside the entity. The structure had worked because the same person carried judgment, authority, and consequence.

When that person died, the structure remained. The assumptions did not.

John leaned back and reread his notes. There was no fraud here. No deception. The exposure was the by-product of trust extended over time and never recalibrated.

He considered how this would sound if explained aloud. Too abstract. Too easily dismissed.

He turned to the share register again. No change. No mechanism for transition. The absence of planning was not a failure of foresight so much as an act of confidence. The man had not believed the question urgent.

John wrote another line.

Continuity assumed; transfer undefined.

By late afternoon, the picture was complete enough to be dangerous.

Selling the business would not extinguish the guarantees. Winding it down would trigger them. Continuing without change would prolong exposure. Expanding would compound it.

There was no path that did not require recognition.

John closed the file and sat for a moment, considering order rather than content. What to present first. What to withhold until asked. How much could be said without overwhelming those who had not chosen this complexity.

He would not editorialise. He would describe.

He gathered the documents into a single stack and placed them in the folder. On the front, he clipped a clean sheet of paper and wrote, in his neat, economical hand:

Founding assumptions no longer hold.

He left the table and went to the sink. The light outside had shifted again, lengthening the day without warming it. The work was no longer about reassurance or caution.

It was about consequence, and how evenly it would be borne.

When he returned, he drafted a short email.

I am ready to meet and discuss what the expanded review shows. Please let me know when you are available.

He sent it, closed the laptop, and did not reopen it.

The Misunderstanding

They met in the same room, at the same table.

The familiarity unsettled Margaret more than she expected. She had thought, briefly, that the setting might soften what was coming. Instead, it made the distance between then and now more apparent.

John arrived with a single folder. He did not place it on the table immediately.

Andrew nodded. Claire sat with her arms folded, listening.

John opened the folder and removed the first document. He did not pass it across.

"I'll begin with how the business was established," he said. "Not because that history is unusual, but because it explains what exists now."

He spoke without emphasis. Dates. Amounts. The progression from initial loan to renewal. The ease with which accommodation had become routine. He described the structure without assigning weight to it.

Margaret followed carefully. She had lived alongside these events, but not inside them.

John paused and looked up. "At no point was ownership shared."

The words landed quietly.

Margaret frowned. "I don't understand."

"You were not a partner," John said. "You were a guarantor."

Andrew shifted. "That can't be right."

John turned a page. "It is."

Margaret shook her head. "I signed everything. We discussed everything."

"I don't doubt that," John said. "But the documents are explicit."

He slid the page toward her.

She did not touch it.

"You guaranteed the loan," John continued. "Jointly and severally. That obligation survives the business. It survives sale. It survives your husband's death."

Margaret looked down at her hands. "So, what was I, then?"

John answered carefully. "You were supporting the business. Not owning it."

"That's a distinction without a difference," Andrew said.

John did not agree or disagree. "It becomes a significant difference when the business changes hands."

Claire leaned forward slightly. "If we sell, the loan is cleared."

"The loan may be," John said. "The guarantees are not extinguished by sale unless the bank agrees to release them."

Margaret looked up. "They would."

John met her gaze. "They have no reason to."

Silence settled.

"I don't understand how this happened," Margaret said. "We built this together."

"You did," John said. "But the structure does not reflect that."

Andrew's voice sharpened. "You're saying my mother has all the risk and none of the benefit."

"I'm saying the risk was always there," John said. "It was simply never tested."

Margaret's expression tightened. "Why would my husband do that?"

John answered evenly. "He may not have thought of it that way. The arrangement worked. There was no incentive to revisit it."

Claire said quietly, "And now?"

"Now," John said, "the assumptions no longer hold."

Margaret picked up the document at last. She read it slowly, then set it back on the table.

"So, if we sell," she said, "I don't walk away."

"No," John said.

"And if we keep going?"

"The exposure continues."

She closed her eyes briefly. "All this time…"

John waited.

Andrew pushed back his chair. "This is technical. We can negotiate."

"You can try," John said. "But you will be negotiating from a different position than your father did."

Margaret looked between them. "You knew this already," she said to John.

"Yes."

"And you didn't tell us."

"I didn't have authority to," John said. "And I wanted to be certain."

She absorbed that, then nodded once.

Claire broke the silence. "So, what do we do?"

John did not answer immediately. He gathered the papers into a neat stack.

"There are options," he said. "Each has a cost."

Margaret's voice was steady now. "Then tell us."

John closed the folder.

"That," he said, "is the next conversation. We'll need time to set it out properly."

Liability

They did not speak again for several days.

John did not chase them. Once information had been placed on the table, the next movement belonged to those who would bear its weight.

When the call came, it was from Claire.

"We need to understand what this means in practice," she said. "Not in theory."

John suggested a time. She agreed without hesitation.

They met in the same room, though the arrangement had shifted. The chairs were no longer evenly spaced. Margaret sat closest to the head of the table. Andrew stood at the window until John began.

"This is not about fault," John said. "It's about attachment."

Andrew turned. "Attachment?"

"Liability," John said. "Where it sits, and when it activates."

He laid out three documents, side by side.

"If the business is sold as it stands," he said, "the loan is repaid. That does not release the guarantee unless the bank agrees. At present, there is no reason for them to do so."

Margaret nodded once. She had already accepted this.

"If the business is wound down," John continued, "the guarantees are called. Timing determines how much."

Andrew frowned. "And if we keep going?"

"The exposure continues," John said. "It does not reduce simply because trading continues."

Claire leaned forward. "So, every option leaves my mother exposed."

"Yes."

"That's unacceptable," Andrew said.

John did not respond.

"What about restructuring?" Claire asked.

John waited a moment before answering. "That depends on what you mean."

"Professional management," she said. "Taking us out of day-to-day control."

"That addresses operational risk," John said. "Not personal exposure."

Margaret spoke for the first time. "Then what does?"

John turned a page.

"Recognition," he said. "Followed by negotiation."

Andrew scoffed. "With the bank?"

"Yes."

"They'll never agree."

"They might," John said. "But not on the basis of sentiment."

Silence followed.

Claire asked, "What does the bank see?"

John answered carefully. "They see a structure that has lost the person they trusted. They see guarantees that remain enforceable. They will wait."

Andrew paced. "So, we have no leverage."

"Not yet," John said.

Margaret looked at him. "What creates it?"

John met her gaze. "Change."

Andrew stopped. "You're saying we need to put something at risk."

"I'm saying the risk already exists," John replied. "What you choose to do determines who carries it."

Claire exhaled slowly. "And if we do nothing?"

John answered without emphasis. "The position worsens quietly."

Andrew laughed once, sharply. "That's not an answer."

"It is," John said. "Just not a comforting one."

Margaret folded her hands. "What would you recommend?"

John shook his head. "I don't recommend courses of action. I explain consequences."

Andrew turned away again.

Claire said, "Then explain the consequence of waiting."

John did not need to consult his notes. "The bank arrangements will continue on existing terms. Exposure remains personal. When the next decision is forced—by market, by equipment failure, by staff—the choice will be narrower and more expensive."

Margaret closed her eyes briefly.

When she opened them, she said, "We can't leave it like this."

Andrew said nothing.

Claire looked at John. "What does continuing your work achieve now?"

"It allows you to negotiate with information," John said. "And to restructure deliberately rather than under pressure."

"And your fee?" Andrew said.

John did not flinch. "It increases."

Claire nodded. "Of course it does."

Margaret said, "Then we need to decide."

John gathered the documents into a neat stack but did not close the folder.

"I won't proceed without instruction," he said. "And I won't dilute what I tell you to make that decision easier."

Andrew looked at his mother. Then at Claire.

The silence stretched, but this time it was not confusion. It was calculation.

At last, Margaret said, "We need help running the business properly."

Andrew stiffened. "You mean handing it over."

"I mean protecting it," she said. "And ourselves."

John watched without intervening.

Claire said, "If we restructure, and bring in professionals, does that help?"

"It creates a basis for release," John said. "Not a guarantee. But a conversation."

Margaret nodded. "Then that's the direction."

Andrew did not argue. He did not agree either.

John closed the folder.

"I'll outline what that entails," he said. "And what it will cost."

They did not ask him to stay.

When John left, the decision was not complete. But it had begun to move.

Interlude — Margaret Alone

The house was quiet again, but it was a different quiet.

Margaret noticed the change most clearly in the mornings. The telephone did not ring. There were no emails asking for clarification, no requests forwarded by Andrew, no documents needing immediate attention. The work had moved elsewhere, leaving her with the residue rather than the momentum.

She made tea and let it cool. She sorted the post and set it aside unread. When she did read it, she did so carefully, as though attention itself carried consequence.

Most of the letters were procedural. Forms acknowledging receipt. Notices of processing. Requests for confirmation that led nowhere in particular. They did not require decisions. They did not invite response.

Margaret placed them in a folder and aligned the edges.

The absence of urgency unsettled her more than its presence ever had.

During the weeks after the meetings ended, she became aware of how often her husband had been the point at which things stopped. Questions had arrived and ended with him. Decisions had been made and absorbed without reverberation. Now, questions passed through her without resolving.

She sat at the dining table and reread the loan documents John had left with her.

Not to find fault. To understand shape.

The dates surprised her. Not because they were unfamiliar, but because they were numerous. The guarantee appeared again and again, renewed in language that was almost identical each time. She had signed without ceremony. The signature was her own, steady and legible. There was no mark of hesitation.

Margaret traced the ink with her finger.

She tried to remember each moment of consent, but there had been no single moment. There had been evenings at the table, papers pushed toward her while the kettle boiled. There had been conversations half-finished, decisions concluded without announcement. She had trusted that what she was supporting was also what she was sharing.

The documents did not reflect that trust.

She realised, with a clarity that surprised her, that consent had accumulated. It had not been given once, decisively, but in increments that felt too small to contest at the time.

Margaret closed the folder and pushed it aside.

Later, she returned to it.

This time, memory intruded more readily. Not scenes, but arrangements. The way her husband spoke of the business as though it were an extension of himself, and the way she had accepted that without resentment. They had divided their lives along lines that felt natural then. He carried the business. She carried the rest.

What she had not carried, she now saw, was authority.

The distinction had not mattered while everything functioned. It mattered now.

Margaret stood and walked through the house. She paused in rooms she had not entered in weeks. The study remained unchanged. Papers stacked where they had been left. The chair pushed back slightly, as though he had intended to return.

She did not sit.

In the following days, Andrew called less often. Claire did not call at all. When they did speak, the conversations were careful, bounded by what had already been said. Preparations were being discussed elsewhere, by advisers and intermediaries not yet formally engaged. Margaret was consulted, but she was not directing.

Understanding, she realised, had not restored agency.

One afternoon, she received a call from the bank. It was brief and courteous. The man on the line confirmed receipt of information and advised that further correspondence would follow. He did not ask questions. He did not offer reassurance.

Margaret thanked him and ended the call.

She sat for a long time afterward, hands folded, aware of the weight of what remained unresolved. The business might change. The structure might shift. But the obligations she had accepted would not dissolve simply because they were now visible.

Margaret understood this without bitterness.

She began to see her position more clearly. Not as victim, and not as partner, but as bearer. The guarantees had not been extracted from her. They had been offered, repeatedly, in good faith.

That did not make them lighter.

In the evening, she wrote a short list. Not of tasks, but of boundaries. Things she would no longer assume. Decisions she would require to be named. The list was not long.

When she finished, she folded the paper and placed it in the drawer beside the telephone.

The house remained quiet.

This time, she did not mistake it for peace.

She understood now that consequence did not announce itself. It waited for acknowledgement and then required accommodation.

She accepted that.

Acceptance, she knew, was often the most difficult part.

Structural Resolution

Terms

The engagement was formalised without ceremony.

The adviser's letter arrived by email first, then by post. It set out scope, authority, and limitation in language that left little room for interpretation. Margaret read it twice before signing. This time, she noted the exclusions as carefully as the permissions.

She signed knowing precisely what the agreement did and did not do.

The authority granted was narrow by design. Decisions would be made elsewhere, but accountability would remain where it already sat. The distinction mattered to her now. It marked the difference between participation and consent.

When she returned the document, she did so promptly. There was no advantage in delay. The work would begin regardless of her readiness.

Reconfiguration

The changes that followed were procedural rather than dramatic.

Meetings were scheduled and minuted. Reports were produced and circulated. The business began to speak in documents rather than conversation. Margaret attended where required and withdrew where she was not.

Andrew resisted at first. Not openly, but through small refusals: questions asked too late, decisions revisited unnecessarily. The behaviour was noted, not challenged. Over time, it diminished.

Claire watched from a distance. She asked questions when invited and declined when she was not. Her detachment was interpreted as pragmatism, which suited everyone.

The premises changed subtly. Notices appeared where familiarity had once sufficed. Procedures replaced habit. The effect was not efficiency so much as containment.

Margaret observed the process without intervening. The business continued to operate. That fact alone felt instructive.

Bank Response

The bank's correspondence acknowledged the changes without comment.

Language shifted slightly. References to history gave way to references to structure. Requests were framed formally and answered in kind. There was no suggestion of release, only recognition.

Margaret understood the message clearly.

Change was noted. It was not rewarded.

The guarantees remained in force. They would remain so until circumstances justified reconsideration. That threshold was undefined.

What Remains

Margaret returned to the house more often now that there was less to attend to elsewhere.

She kept the documents in order. She answered correspondence when required. The exposure had not lifted, but it had become bounded by understanding.

The business continued under management that did not require her presence. That absence felt deliberate rather than imposed.

One evening, she took the list from the drawer beside the telephone and read it again. The boundaries she had written were still intact. She folded the paper and returned it to its place.

Nothing had been resolved. Much had been clarified.

Margaret accepted that this was the shape of the future: narrower than before but no longer obscured by assumption.

She switched off the light and left the room.

Coda

John closed the file knowing it would not be the last time he saw this configuration. The elements were familiar now: a death, a guarantee, a family who discovered too late that understanding did not equate to control. He had recognised the pattern before—not always in his own work, sometimes only in fragments, in correspondence or passing references that never quite resolved into cases. The advice was always sound. The timing never was. As he filed the papers away, John noted—not for the record, just for himself—that the work was no longer about prevention. It was about explaining damage that had already settled, quietly, into place.

Within Scope

The papers arrived on a Tuesday, bundled more carefully than necessary. Buckland noted this without interest. Some people believed neatness signalled seriousness. Others simply disliked disorder. Either way, the contents were predictable.

He logged the engagement, skimmed the covering letter, and placed the file at the back of the tray. There was no urgency implied, and none required. The matter concerned a proposed restructuring, internal to a group whose governance arrangements had been revised twice in the past decade. His role was limited to advising on a narrow point of interpretation. Nothing more.

By midweek he had read the background material. It was competent, if selective. He made a note to request one additional document, not because it was strictly necessary, but because its absence created a slight asymmetry. He sent the request and turned to other work.

The document arrived the following morning. It did not contradict anything already provided. It did, however, sit awkwardly alongside it.

Buckland did not immediately identify why. He read it twice, then set it aside and continued with his draft opinion. Only later, while re-reading a paragraph he had already marked as complete, did he recognise the source of the discomfort. The issue was not in what the document said, but in what it assumed.

The assumption was reasonable. It was also fragile.

He revised the paragraph to ensure it answered only the question he had been asked. The wording tightened. The scope narrowed. The conclusion remained unchanged.

When he finished, he leaned back slightly, hands resting on the desk, and considered whether anything further was required. There was an alternative phrasing he could have used—less direct, perhaps more suggestive—but it would have implied a concern not formally raised. He deleted it.

The opinion was sent that afternoon.

A week later, a courtesy email arrived acknowledging receipt. It thanked him for his clarity. There was no request for elaboration.

In the days that followed, Buckland found himself thinking again about the document he had requested. Not because it undermined his advice, but because it clarified how the advice would be used. He did not regret the opinion. It was correct. He did not believe a different conclusion was warranted.

What unsettled him was something else: the recognition that, had he been asked a slightly different question, his answer would have been materially different.

No such question came.

Several weeks later, the matter appeared briefly in an industry circular. The restructuring had proceeded as anticipated. There was no controversy attached to it, no dissent reported. The language used to describe the decision echoed phrases from his opinion, though not verbatim.

Buckland read the notice once and moved on.

At the end of the month, he closed the file. The billing was routine. The internal checklist showed all steps complete. There were no outstanding actions.

Before archiving the documents, he opened the draft email he had saved and never sent. He read it carefully. It raised no objections and offered no conclusions. It merely pointed to an alignment issue that might, in another context, have warranted discussion.

He deleted it.

The file was archived. The system confirmed closure.

Buckland turned to the next matter in the tray.

www.ingramcontent.com/pod-product-compliance
Lightning Source LLC
Chambersburg PA
CBHW061452210726
48287CB00007B/2477